F. Roena Medini

**Love's Hymnal**

F. Roena Medini

**Love's Hymnal**

ISBN/EAN: 9783744766852

Printed in Europe, USA, Canada, Australia, Japan

Cover: Foto ©Andreas Hilbeck / pixelio.de

More available books at **www.hansebooks.com**

# LOVE'S HYMNAL

## *SONNETS*

BY

### F. ROENA MEDINI

# LOVE'S HYMNAL

## Sonnets

BY

F. ROENA MEDINI

CAMBRIDGE, MASS.
1896

*The Riverside Press, Cambridge, Mass., U. S. A.*
Electrotyped and Printed by H. O. Houghton & Co.

TO

MY HUSBAND

HENRY JERROLD CASEDY

LOVE'S Hymnal this, as found on Cupid's
    pyre,
Where burned the hearts of hopeless manhood
        — age ;
These tender plaints, this closely written page
Illumined by the gleaming flames of fire,
Burned not away, but sang its song to lyre
Attuned to simple lay.   O'erlooked by sage,
A throbbing heart there paused, as if to gauge
The pains of others with its own, — as dire
Misfortune ever turns to like for aid
In time of need, — best comforted to find
That others' pains are keener than their own.
Some comfort here the lover found, nor stayed
To quench the flame that round the altar twined,
And love hath since far dearer grown.

# Love's Hymnal

## I

MY love, my better self, read line on line, —
It is my soul that speaks, so, dear, fold
down
The leaves I send, to be my heart's renown.
Within the temple of thy heart, if mine
Hath raised with others there a holy shrine,
Am I to hush my whispered prayer, or drown
With tears the arches high, at love's mute frown?
If there an alien I should prove, Oh! twine
The altar I have raised with chaplets fair,
To be my tomb, and love the grave that none
Shall see, for love's dear sake.  Imprisoned there
I still shall live as memory lives, to shine
Adown the pathway of thy life's decline,
Till out of death, again life's victory 's won.

1

## II

I F my poor heart leaps forth in rhythmed line,
   And lips dare breathe what fluttering heart-
      throbs tell,
Think not the utterance came at birth, — or fell
From lips unwittingly.   Long time the sign
I strove to stifle in my breast, — the wine
That ferments in the darkness of its cell
Is not at times more bitter in its well
Than I, denouncing this mad love of mine.
The wondering world would say, full well I know,
If once it read the passion of my soul,
" 'T were late," but not for torturing pains that
      grow
To tempests that o'erwhelm like bitter fate. —
*With weary brow and heavy feet, the goal*
*I sought is known and reached, alas, too late.*

## III

AND if thy beating heart the truth tells not,
Believe no words of mine.   Or if they start
No echoing sigh, compassion's weary part
I would not ask of thee.   Such mournful lot
Were sadder than these heavy tears that blot
The page whereon I write.   If thy warm heart
Be dumb to throbbing of my own, apart
From tender pity that some need begot,
I am no more to thee than yonder moon
That, why, thou canst not tell, within thy breast
A sadness drops, that passes ere 't is noon.
I am no more than they, once friends, who 've
            learned
Thy bitterness through trust betrayed, — more
            blest
I 'd be by far, to know my friendship spurned.

3

## IV

SINCE halting verse hath breathed this secret care,
Mine eyes refuse to master thine.  One time,
I held thee so — aloof, and deemed it crime
In that my pulse beat high, but now I dare
Not stir the bubble of a thought, aware
We both must strive for mastery to climb
To summit of a life we'd make sublime.
And so, when thy dear eyes seek mine, I share
With thee thy thought, yet will not look to read
Thy heart's desire, lest that my lips lean hence
To drink sweet nectar with true lovers' greed.
Sternly I set our task with Art above
All else, and hold in leash each quivering
        sense,
To meet thy glance and chain with duty — love.

## V

NOT joy, the cymbals strike to sound my
   heart.
To hymn my thoughts, is bitterness the meed,
Some sharply darting pain, the birth's sad need :
Some growing doubt, that I who stand apart
To catch the glow of morn, denying Art,
Have reached too far, and so must stand indeed
With empty hands, which, pricked with thorns,
   do bleed.
But I, that, gazing, felt the poisoned dart
Sped from thine eyes, had gladly swooned with
   pain,
When trembling fear I had not read aright
Crept in to strike a chill through every vein.
And yet love turned no brighter page of fate
*Than just to love thee.   I, to morning light*
*Awoke too soon, — and thou, awoke too late.*

## VI

NO vain desire speeds with the flash of wit,
    The sympathies that reaching out gain
        friends,
Till 'round my woman's shrine, there kneeling
        bends
A goodly company where queen I sit.
Each conquest made, on memory's tablet writ,
Is thought of thee, and added lustre lends
To prove, in pleasing others, that amends
It makes for pleasing thee, and if I flit,
A restless bird, what better proof is thine
Than that my heart, oft sad, its time beguiles?
If changed (I know the art), thou ne'er shalt
        see
How deeply I may grieve.  The bitter brine
Of tears unshed, I 'll hide beneath the smiles
The world found glad, because beloved by thee.

## VII

LAST night I sat amidst a gallant throng
When suddenly, my love, thou cam'st to me
In thought! Thy presence, thou, electric — thee,
In plenitude of will, as forceful, strong.
Thy melting eye held mine a moment long,
No more; yet in that instant all to thee
Had yielded sway, and faint, I could not see
The surging faces of the crowd. The song
A graceful singer sang, I had not heard.
Beside me, some one spoke, and marveled much
At pallor of my face; I spoke no word,
But wanly smiled. The spell, alas, was broke.
A dream — you were not there, and oft from such
A vision, sweet with pain, I am awoke.

## VIII

DEAR heart, I dare not dream of what our lives
Might be, if we were free to love, we two,
As freely as the earth loves sun, the dew
The flowers, — when at thy fancied coming strives
The soul for mastery, and almost rives
In twain the body and its sense.   To thee
Grants God my ardent soul enslaved, and free
Or bound, as thine, nor life nor death deprives.
What then, if through the temple of the soul
(Made meek by blights mankind can only guess)
There shone a hope that heart to heart our years
Might drift to peaceful calm — that tangled mesh
Of life unraveled, swift to us appears
The blessed haven of that longed for goal.

## IX

IN loving thee a little, can it harm ? "
  Saidst thou ?  The guerdon of a love is won
By risking all, by giving all.   Not one
In this wide world hath loved, if love's alarm
Held Cupid's bow in bondage, or the warm
And beating heart its mercury limits run.
To flee, to' crowd out thought, if it be done
And so to " little love " be dwarfed, we arm
The will and teach the heart, through chill of
      world's
Calm reasoning, that love can buy or this,
Or that, where Fate rules all.   When she unfurls
The scroll whereon is writ thy name and mine,
Shall we there find a withered rose to kiss
With tears, or deathless tendrils, love doth twine ?

## X

WHEN first the fingers of our hands had yet
But touched, I felt from thine electric stream
Like lava through each limb.  My thoughts which teem
With fancies, much I blamed, and strictly set
Unbending watch o'er folly, which, to let
Unchidden go, disgraced, I thought, the dream
I held of noble womanhood.   The beam
Of thy soft eye with loyalty I met.
My duty done, no thought could e'er intrude ;
Yet when emotion in our hearts awoke
Again, I chided mine, and said : " Be still,
There 's danger here for him.  My sufferings rude
Must not o'ercast his spirit 'gainst my will."
And so, my heart I on my honor broke.

## XI

WHEN intuition taught me that to gain
  Sweet peace, thy heart waged struggles
    fierce, there waked
No thought of self.   For thee my peace was
    staked,
As guerdon of the wish to save you pain.
But what of self?   I sought the path in vain.
When o'er my lips the anxious flood escaped
In sentences half formed, or voice enlaked
In tears, that years of grief had left like rain,
Unwept, thine eyes, true mirrors of thy soul,
Cried out to me, "Thou for thyself dost plead."
But when my lips had tremblingly turned mute,
Thou saidst, "Give speech unto our souls, to roll
The stone away and chide, is like a lute,
And sweet as praise, what wots if I take heed."

## XII

TO chide I feared, for in my heart there grew
    So swift a consciousness of love, — delayed
Till now, I shrank within my soul dismayed,
And coldness barred my heart from self, till
      through
The weary hours of night, no mother knew
More holy longings, nor more humbly prayed,
Than I for thee, whate'er thy life essayed.
Again we stand unveiled to each, and true
As magnets, sweep our souls in one, for time
Eternal, and through space. Yet, gathering force,
We utter words belying speech of eyes :
Our honor staked 'gainst love, we know no course
Beside, and bondsmen to ourselves, arise
To stem the passion of a love sublime.

## XIII

WHAT though my pulses thrilled like mighty flame,

That seething round half blinded me, I held
At bay the prayer within thine eyes, — impelled
By powers above, beyond — who knows? (The same

Hath guided us o'er pitfalls deep, we came
Upon all unaware, when, still upheld
By powers unseen, the raging storm is quelled,
Before we 've asked for strength through heavenly name.)

In vain! I stood confessed unto my soul,
That nothing stood between my life and thee,
But just so much of doubt that might be sin,
To give thus much, were meant to give the whole,
And then no more to self, denied, "to be"
Was written on my heart, and burned therein.

## XIV

WHAT greeting shall be given thee, my
    own,
When, listening rapt, I hear thy step, and think
That all the world has heard the sound to link
Its bounding echo with my changèd tone?
Shall I so steel my looks that thou alone
Canst note the blood from out my lips doth
    sink
To level of my heart, and o'er its brink
The throbs rebound till, 'gainst my temples
    grown
To thousand anvils, I but hear my voice
An icy tone, that utters civil words
In phrases rounded well for other ears?
So, greeting thee, my inward sense as birds
Made tremulous, there rests no other choice,
And opposite of that I am, appears.

## XV

OR if thy coming find me quite alone,
  And, unaware, I ope the door to find
Thee there enframed, and flame of joy behind
The slower courtesy of speech, upthrown,
Leaps forth from shining eyes, they swift atone
By hiding in such offices the mind
Conceives to mask itself, — a spool to wind,
To drape a curtain, — this or that, till grown
More calm, mine eyes can look in thine and
    speak
Of trivial things, as if 't were they, not thee,
Made up my sum of life, — or else, turned weak,
I scarcely dare give speech, lest lips too bold
Such truths shall yield, I stand unveiled,
    and be
Unworthy thee, and all thy heart may hold.

## XVI

WHEN oft the longing  for thy presence sweeps
Like chilly blast across my aching heart,
And, throbbing to its core, all else is part
Of chaos, standing still in icy deeps
Of space, wherein Time's dial mutely weeps,
Refusing more to move, since we apart
Must stand, — in visions comest thou, to start
The universe in rhythmic beat, . . . upleaps
My soul to rest in thine its piteous care,
And once again, by vision pacified,
I mingle with the world, speak light, am gay,
And teach my heart it illy does to wear
A grief that burns earth's uses from my day, —
But swift returned, my grief is magnified.

## XVII

WHAT though thy tenderness like cloak enfold
Me round, and soft as dew thy kisses fall
Upon my face? my doubting heart must call
It pity's proof, not love's, thy heart doth hold,
Lest ardor of my own, which, grown too bold,
Interpretations make, and wrong to all
The rarer tenderness thy speech let fall,
Begot by no such flame as mine, — if told
At morn, at noon, at night thy love, — if held
The idol of thy heart, I still these fears
Must court, that, self-deceived, thou lov'dst me
          not.
And so, 't is best this love of mine (impelled
As flowers to hide when noonday's sun appears),
Beyond the joy of loving thee, — asks nought.

## XVIII

WHEN first my mocking lips were brushed
  by thine
More soft than breezes kiss the flowers at morn,
I know not how my life awoke newborn ;
Within thy arms, thy lips enshrined in mine,
I had forgot, and blushed, that, like a vine,
I clung to thee as if to part had torn
Love's rapture from my heart.  So long I 'd worn
The mask indifference, that to now incline
My head unto thy will, and on thy breast
To sudden trembling take, was yielding quite.
But brief such dream to woman, who awakes
To danger of her love.   For her the test,
To rise to strength, and from such joy take flight.
For her is left the pain brief rapture makes.

18

## XIX

AT Venice, in the centuries now past,
    Near entrance to the Doge's palace, stood
A lion, 'twixt whose lips, for worldly good,
The people placed each plaint or prayer. . . .
        Thou, cast
Before the palace of my heart, as fast
The secrets, mute as he, receiv'st my brood
Of plaints, my vows, my prayers, that, often sued,
Outnumber drops within the ocean vast.
Swift on thy ruby lips with blessings kissed
Is laid my prayer, with repetitions soft,
And then I speed away with guilty face,
As they, too, sped from urgent prayer, which oft
Had wronged their gracious rights withal ; but
        list,
Still unrepentant, here my prayer I place.

## XX

WHEN once thy hand outreached sought
  mine, awaked
By tenderness, my own poor hand crept in,
And like a rose with folded leaves, its thin
And taper fingers, that full long had ached
To know such loving joy, lay still and slaked
Their burning thirst for loving touch therein,
Till, pulses calmed, no fluttering bird within
Its nest could fold its weary wings (though
  waked
Ere dawn) with gentler restfulness.   My hand
Since then hath grown more gentle to mankind,
Hath seemed as if for lofty purpose planned.
In other grasp it hath not long remained,
As if once sanctified, it shrank to find
Itself in heedless clasp o'ermuch detained.

## XXI

WHEN first I knew thee, swiftly words of
     praise
My lips would pass, as men give praise to
     men; —
Or women, each to each, now and again
Will frankly praise a son's, a father's ways,
Quite innocent of deeper sense than weighs
Beneath our idlest words.   I found that when
We least expect, love's fetters hide, and then
Are welded fast through all our future days.
Since when, I scarce can say thy name, so fast
My pulses bound, and others chance in speech
To say or this, or that of thee. — To frame
Thy praise I coldly speak, or seek to cast
Aside the consciousness of love, to reach
That calm control indifference may claim.

## XXII

THOU hast assured me oft I need not fear
    Thy loss, and yet, 'twixt thought and
      speech there lies
The subtle field interpretation. — Wise
And chosen words mislead the heart, a tear
Belies a phrase, and so, grown glad while near,
When gone, swift fears that I mistook thee rise
Like haunting ghosts, and then within me dies
The comfort thou hadst left. My duty clear,
Again I chide my heart for loving thee,
Lest that I lay upon thy spirit aught
Of weight that draws unto itself a sigh,
A tear, nay any melancholy thought
That might in loving service, bold and free,
More happily be given were I not nigh.

## XXIII

IF I do wrong my love and thee, to sow
Such unbelief, an abnegation this
Of love's great joy, — sorely its good I miss ;
Yet, placing far away the hopes, 't is so
An adamantine wall 'gainst bitterer blow
Of disappointment.  But I love thee, — kiss
Thee as my spirit's good, and feel such bliss
Must overtop by far a worldly show
Of reasoning.  I love thee !  Love thou me.
But love me as thou lov'st the sun, — no less
Thine own, if missed a day, and wakes no fear
Its beams will fail to shine again on thee.
Or, love me as thou lov'st the stars, that, near
Or far, do glow with tender watchfulness.

## XXIV

AND how, my heart of hearts, shall I love
  thee?
What plenitude of words could tell thee how,
And never falter, never err.  I vow
My love, and yet the pictured speech, I see
When done, hath outlined merely.  Drawn as
      free
As artist's hand, but still I must allow
'T would fit a hundred loves that humbly bow
Before the throne of Cupid.  Mine must be
I know not what, — the gladness of the spheres,
The sadness of the grave, — the light of heaven,
The pains of hell.  The joyous laugh, — the tears
That ope the floodgates of the soul, the songs
Of tenderness and mirth, the fears that leaven
Every bliss, and trust which rights all wrongs.

## XXV

I LOVE thee with the childlike faith of one
Believing God, — with purity that shines
Above an angel's brow ; with love that binds
Our hearts in simpler deeds of life, that run
On level of its arduous duties done. —
Its talks, its walks, the glance, the sigh, it finds
Swift sympathies in each. — A love that blinds
Us so, we scarce beneath its dazzling sun
Can choose the path, for O, I love thee too
With woman's struggling heart, whom love doth
   wound
Till oft she falters o'er the brink of wrong
For him who doth her heart's desire imbue,
And right for God. What more but to be strong ?
For love debased, alas, is love uncrowned.

## XXVI

IN all the years I lived, not knowing thee,
  Amidst my griefs there dwelt a soulful sight,
Upholding me as one that seeth a light.
There waked no sound, unthrilled from thee to
    me,
No sadness could I know, that 'neath it, free
As chimes of bells, did not thy coming bright
Ring out.   How could my griefs bring blight
When it was writ thy light mine eyes should
    see !                    .
Philosophy hath bitter laws; we grow,
And reach, and yearn for what we scarcely know ;
Then Cupid, perching unaware, his tip
Speeds forth, to shatter castles high as air.
So strong, grave science hath no art nor care
To fill, yet Cupid's bow the whole can trip.

## XXVII

WHEN, years agone, a sudden conscious
    thought
Passed through thy mother's heart th' unwritten
    word,
I bless the quickened pulse that in her stirred
The knowledge of thy sacred charge, which
    naught
But God's own will could her gainsay; where
    aught
That blessed or beautified her sight, or bird
That soared, each glorious song or sound she
    heard
Was cherished for the sake of life she sought
To nourish with her being's tenderest care.
I bless her for her daily thoughts that grew
To hopeful love; I bless her for the dreams
She wove into the garb she 'd have thee wear.
I can but think, of all the brood she knew,
Thy advent, rich with love, the dearest seems.

27

## XXVIII

I LOVE the earth whereon thy shadow 's laid,
The sun that kisses thee, the moon that
   peeps
Into the casement where my loved one sleeps.
I love the book wherein the letters fade
That bear the name thy boyish fingers made.
I love the ivory which forever keeps
The impress of thy staying touch, or leaps
'Neath mine to hopeful sounds, when, sore afraid,
I sighed that only these remain to me.
I love a voice in certain tearful song,
Grown sacred since one day it spoke of thee.
And should the grave cast o'er thee noisome
      breath,
I 'd love the mound that sheltered thee, and long
To meet, while blessing it, th' embrace of death.

## XXIX

I BLESS the maidens who have loved thee well,
(I cannot blame the ones who tempted thee).
Each rose-leaf round thy footsteps cast must be
The memories tender, whose sweet perfume tell
The fateful, dearest love that thee befell,
Was *last* among the roses on its tree.
It with rare fragrance hung there lovingly,
A little shook by storms that sweep the dell,
A trifle pale from tears the night doth start ;
But when, at look of thine, it blushed again,
New life suffused its ardent veins, and leaf
By leaf the history of sweet love's belief
Is written softly there, with Cupid's dart,
And waits alone for thy dear heart's *Amen.*

## XXX

IF these my written words, with love aglow,
  Were all that in thy life remained of me,
I wonder if thy heart, at last set free,
Might not forget?   Then be it so!
What greater praise than that the notes that grow
More sweet with love awake thy heart, and be
Forgot the singer, not the song?   When we
Give love, and ask no counterpart, we know
The joy of worship is our recompense.
When joy's sweet pain outlives its parent stem,
As must the thorn outlive the fragrant rose,
Full oft the fragrance o'er our dreaming sense
Will swift recall the happier day, and so
Be born that perfect peace, love's diadem.

## XXXI

IF I remained content to hear thy name,
To see thee pass afar, though thou mightst
    yearn
To see my face, thou soon unmoved wouldst turn
Away without a sigh.   It is the same
With graves we pass each day: when sorrow
    came,
The mourner grieved; accustomed grief will burn
And sear the heart, till much alike, we learn,
Is sad indifference, which, to gentler frame,
We call the " healing o'er of time."   Farewell !
Necessity to part is ever sad,
Yet worse the love that of the grave hath breath.
So then I flee, when to have stayed, with glad
And tender touches of thy hand to tell
Of love, were bliss ; to go, *a living death.*

## XXXII

ALAS, alas, for youth's dear sake, I ought
Not sing such sad refrain, but guide my
song
Until, triumphant, it might ring so strong
That heaven would echo to the gladness caught.
No life so sad it hath not light inwrought
With sombre woof ; no heart so dead, the wrong
It suffered may not hope reward.   The long
And dreary road hath aye an end, and, sought
Or anxiously evaded, death will free
The soul from endless striving 'gainst a fate
We vainly seek through life to subjugate,
With hope to grow in attributes, that, done
With earth, the higher joys of heaven will be
Conceded recompense for perils run.

## XXXIII

I WONDER, if beholding me thus worn
    And shaken with the weary years, a tear
Will not, beneath thine eyelids, dim thy dear
And kindly sight ; and if so loved, though born
To less of joy than all the world, my torn
And bleeding heart were not repaid the fear
It held, by thee forgot, that year by year
Must heavier prove than could be easy borne?
Nay, nay, I would not have thy love at cost
So dear to thee ; that I be tempest-toss'd,
It is enough, and better far the thought,
To stand aside, if thou wert passing by,
To gather to my heart the pain it brought,
Remain unseen, and bless thee with each sigh.

## XXXIV

ONE time I thought, when griefs grew old, my face
Would claim again its tender outlines, glow
With all the light that once reflected so
The happiness within ; for oft the grace
Of years may softer beauty interlace
Than youth hath ever known ; but though my woe
Be banished from my face, and waking grow
To brightness with the interests of our race,
Asleep, the angel Sorrow draws her lines
Deep in wherever she hath cast her shade,
And only grief remains.   At morn the brines
Of bitter tears hath washed therein so deep,
Nor youth nor hope, one vestige more doth keep,
And joy handmaiden of dire woe is made.

## XXXV

WHEN some one spake thy name, to say,
    " He comes,"
My soul took courage ; yet, last night, so dark
The way, I wondered how, with not a spark
Of light about my path, no meagre crumbs
Of comfort, I could bear this grief that numbs
The heart to common joy.  Death, grim and
    stark,
Holds not the dread that loveless life doth mark
The years withal ; so, when they said, " He
    comes,"
I joyed, although I wished my weary face
Might be forever hid, as one long dead :
Remembered ever with its youth, its light,
And rosy tints ; remembered with no trace
Of age or care ; beloved because so bright,
Not cherished for the beauty that has fled.

## XXXVI

IN all the shipwrecks of earth's stormy life,
  Thine eyes still beam the beacon o'er its sea.
When others fail, thou, steadfast, art to me
God's truth, the gleam of sun that 'midst the
      strife
Doth light my path when bitter doubts are rife.
When all seems false and hollow, then I see
Thy face, I feel thy touch, and know in thee
Those virtues which true manhood claims ; thy
      life
The one just thing that weary days have known,
The rest as false as happiness we dress
The face withal, or smiles one scatters round
To hide the wounds that bleed within, now grown
Too old and deep for surgeon's knife to sound.
I thank thee, love, for Faith's sweet happiness.

## XXXVII

WHEN through me thrilled the conscious-
      ness of power
To move in thee emotions that thy glance
Alone could wake, I shuddered at the chance
Temptation, seeking to dispel the hour
Of glamour which too ardent souls o'erpower,
I scarce dared touch thy hand when in the dance
We moved to rhythm sweet that e'er enhanced
The wondrous charm. " Not love, true love, my
      dower,
How could he find in this world-beaten shell
The ideal love a poet seeks ?  I wield
Some power, perhaps," I mused, " yet time would
      tell
How fleeting transient passion's reign can be,"
And worldly wise, I saw, but would not yield ;
Yet futile all my struggles to be free !

## XXXVIII

FOR when we sing I see the blood recede
 From out thy face, my own to follow it,
A-vibrate with the thrilling tones that flit
From note to note, soul-stirred by words that
 lead
To sense of sad farewell.   The sudden need
Of strength breaks o'er my heart.   Aroused, I
 sit,
Thy critic stern, — a word, rebuke, admit
No faltering, till back we 're swept and freed
From slumbering passion that would overleap
Control.   O dreaming  hearts,  back,  back  to
 earth,
Hypocrisy, to falsehood, which sweet eyes
Gainsay, but spell me not with lovers' sighs
To ask if I do love, or else I keep
The truth in leash, denying Cupid's birth!

## XXXIX

I SAID, "To part is better for us both ; "
Yet, love, while granting danger, great to
  thee,
What boon in all this life is left to me
So sweet as tender love, whose daily growth
I battled with all laws of mind, and loath
To yield e'en then, I fled because, to see
Thee knowing it a wrong, could never be,
The purer love we 'd choose to give in oath.
Is it enough that thou canst see beneath
This outward form of me some flame
Akin to thine, though worlds would mate us not ?
If sometimes selfish earth's desires bequeath
The pains of longings vain, they only came
To prove (when overcome) their blessed lot.

## XL

THE joyous bells of hope and deathless love
   Are waked this morn to sound such ring-
      ing songs,
I scarce can spell the one that most belongs
To calmer beat of love's repose.   Above
Their broken music, like a restful dove,
My heart in gladness sweet with memory throngs,
Forgetting quite the bitterness and wrongs
That Fate heaped high to check true love.
Mine own, when glad I read the crowded page
Whereon thy love and hopelessness doth wage,
I am not saddened by the maze of pain
That tripped our wary feet ; if they deceived
Two earnest hearts, 't is past, and ours the gain,
Believing, and regretting not that we believed.

## XLI

WHEN thou art nigh, I have no words, no speech,
For swiftly chasing thoughts; I only know
That thou art mine for space so brief, I throw
Away much tender joy within my reach,
In dread of that grim spectre who to each
Will swiftly come and say, "'T is time to go."
And then, thou gone, my thoughts with tumult
      grow
To words I might have said when eyes could
      teach
My meaning, or thy lips with swifter kiss
Had sealed my own with "Yes, I understand."
O love, my king, thou knowest this, all this,
That love is deathless 'midst the chaos life.
Nor reasoning cold, philosophy, nor strife
Can bury love, or love withstand.

## XLII

DOUBT thou a love that fears the sun,
   Or shames itself to speak thus heart to
     heart,
But not of love that hath no thought apart
From thee. Each heart-beat of the past was
     one
Of longing for the joy that is, — we run
The gauntlet of emotions that up start
Alert to recognize dear Cupid's dart,
But how atone for wrong that has been done
When errant Fancy left sore wounds behind?
Let cautiousness o'ermatch the cunning jade, —
If we mistook for love her thin disguise.
Evaded and unsought came love when Cupid
     blind,
Unmindful of his mark, the murderer played
And pinioned us, midst tears and sighs.

## XLIII

AS on the threshold of fruition sweet,
    I pause, and question yet, if right toward
        thee,
How stubborn dual egos are to free
From doubt the aye and nay my heart must
    meet.
Can love's great boon be realized, nor fleet
The happiness once disbelieved? In fee,
One might accept a taste of joy; but see
The goal too dear to hope in dreams, I greet
Its semblance with a doubt.
                                        Forgive, O love,
Long time it is, since in the spirit, thine
I vowed myself, take also thou the blame
Of holding me, as I hold thee. The dove
Of Peace, in loving trust, our hearts shall tame,
And earth a heaven become in life's decline.

## XLIV

LOVE wedded, adds to sleep the blissful
    sense
Of Presence, and the heart o'er-full oft wakes
To joy in joy, or midway slumb'ring, takes
A gladsome comfort stretching thence
A hand inertly, sleepily where dense
The darkness lies, to touch, as light as flakes
Of snow, the dear one's cheek, who mayhap,
    wakes,
Or, sleeping still, imprints the seal intense
Of lips' devotion, or detains the hand
With loving replications of its touch,
As if to say, " God bless thee, dear, 't is planned
That sleeping, waking, or in death, thus much
Thou knowest well, through this unerring bond,
Shall each to each our soul's pure love respond."

## XLV

AND I, grown fonder with the years and thee,
Must wonder that the dial Time, so swift
With griefs for others, yet has left no rift
In summer of our hearts.  I feared to be
Content ; to find myself thus truly free
To love, and be so loved.  That I may lift
A thankful heart, receive the treasured gift
And call it wholly mine, is marvel glad,
And so I hold my happiness in trust,
Half fearing that, like angel visitant,
It prove as brief.  This joy, if I make sad
With less than heaven's confidence, I must
Deny its God and sin, — a militant.